Herman Melville's

Moby Dick

Adapted and illustrated by

Rod Espinosa

magic wagon

visit us at
www.abdopublishing.com

Published by Magic Wagon, a division of the ABDO Publishing Group, 8000 West 78th Street, Edina, Minnesota 55439.

Printed in the United States of America, North Mankato, Minnesota.

Original novel by Herman Melville
Adapted and illustrated by Rod Espinosa
Colored and lettered by Rod Espinosa
Edited by Stephanie Hedlund
Interior layout and design by Antarctic Press
Cover art by Rod Espinosa
Cover design by Neil Klinepier

Library of Congress Cataloging-in-Publication Data

Espinosa, Rod.
Moby Dick / Herman Melville; adapted and illustrated by Rod Espinosa.
p. cm. -- (Graphic classics)
ISBN 978-1-60270-051-2
1. Graphic novels. I. Melville, Herman, 1819-1891. Moby Dick. II. Title.

PN6727.E86E87 2008
741.5'973--dc22

2007012068

012008
062010

TABLE of CONTENTS

Chapter 1 Ishmael

I NEED A ROOM, PLEASE.
WE'RE OUT OF ROOMS, BUT I CAN BUNK YOU UP WITH SOMEONE ELSE.
The inn was filthy, but I had no other choice.
YOUR ROOMMATE IS OUT SELLING HIS HEAD.
HIS WHAT!?
DON'T YA WORRY.
HE'S FROM THE SOUTH SEAS AND SELLS SHRUNK'N HEADS.
That worried me, but it did not concern the innkeeper. He only cared about getting his rent.

I finally got a glimpse of the stranger, and he looked like a savage. Fear ran through my veins!
He pulled an ax from his bag.
AHHHH!
I knew he intended to make me one of his shrunken heads!
WHOO-ES-EE, IS EE THE DEBIL?
DON'T WORRY, NOBODY IS GONNA HURT NOBODY.
YOU DIDN'T TELL ME HE WAS A CANNIBAL! LOOK AT THAT AX!

HA...HA...ME SMOKE-E
That rested my fears...slightly.
Queequeg and I actually started to become friends. He told me he was a prince on his island but had begged to join a whaling boat.
He wanted to bring wonders back to his people.
I started to teach him how to read and about book printing.
Holy Bible

Chapter 2 The Whaling Ship Pequod

WELCOME. I'M CAPTAIN PELEG, ONE OF THE OWNERS OF THE SHIP.
MY FRIEND AND I ARE LOOKING FOR WORK.
WHAT IN THE WORLD!? A CANNIBAL! WE CAN'T ACCEPT HIM. HE'S PROBABLY NOT EVEN CHRISTIAN!
HE BELONGS TO THE CHURCH OF THE WORLD, THAT WE ALL HAPPEN TO WORSHIP IN.
GOOD SERMON, MY BOY, BUT CAN HE FISH?

Queequeg jumped on the bow of the ship and proved his abilities!
YOU SEE HIM SMALL DROP TAR ON WATER DERE?
IF DAT WHALE-E EYE, DAD WHALE-E IT DEAD.
WELCOME TO OUR CREW. WE'LL GET THE PAPERS TOGETHER.
WHO IS THE CAPTAIN OF THE SHIP?
YOU'LL BE WORKING WITH CAPTAIN AHAB.
GET YOUR AFFAIRS IN ORDER. WE SHIP OUT SOON.

HO! MY NAME IS ELIJAH. DID... DID YOU JUST SIGN ONTO THAT SHIP?
YES, WE DID. WHAT IS IT TO YOU?
YOU JUST SOLD YOUR SOUL TO OLD THUNDER... CAPTAIN AHAB!

We walked away from this crazy man. However, it stuck in my mind that his name was Elijah. And Elijah was the prophet in the Bible who predicted many bad things to come.

Chapter 3 The Unseen Captain

We set sail from Nantucket.
We had traveled for some days.
I still had not seen the captain.
TOK THUD
TOK THUD
TOK THUD
Then one day…

Captain Ahab finally appeared! He had an ivory peg replacing his right leg. He also appeared troubled.
GATHER THE MEN! I HAVE SOMETHING TO SAY.
MEN, I KNOW WE ARE LOOKING FOR WHALES. BUT THERE IS ONE IN PARTICULAR I WANT TO FIND.
AND THE ONE WHO SPOTS HIM WILL GET THIS GOLD COIN!

IT'S A WHITE-HEADED WHALE WITH A CROOKED JAW AND A WRINKLED BROW. ONE WITH THREE HOLES PUNCHED IN ITS STARBOARD FLUKE.

WHOEVER SIGHTS IT GETS THIS OUNCE OF SPANISH GOLD.
IT WAS THAT WHALE THAT GAVE ME THIS STUMP.

"WE HAD CHASED THE WHALE AROUND THE CAPE OF GOOD HOPE. IT APPEARED TO RUN FROM US, BUT THEN TURNED AROUND AND ATTACKED OUR BOATS."
"I TRIED TO STAB THE HEART OF THAT WHALE, AND THAT IS WHEN IT GOT MY LEG."

Chapter 4 Captain Ahab's Quest

We quickly caught up to the whale. It was a sperm whale.
Sperm whales were ideal to get because they had spermaceti in their oil. This was used to light lamps and make perfumes.
Our harpoons made quick work of the whale.
We proudly brought our prize back to the ship.

The whale then needed to be stripped of its blubber.

One whale could get us 100 barrels of oil.

Whaling wasn't without its dangers. Many times, men would have to be saved from falling overboard.

One time, a whale's head fell with Tashtego still in it! He was trying to retrieve the case, which is part of the whale head that holds oil.

Queequeg, without any regard for his own life, dove overboard to save him.

Chapter 5 Strange Omens

One of the crew, named Fedallah, was a strange sort. Many thought he was the devil. He had a strange relationship with the captain.
I HAD A VISION, A VISION OF HOW YOU WILL DIE.
REALLY?
YOU WILL DIE BY THE ROPE.
BY A HANGING? THAT WILL NEVER HAPPEN.

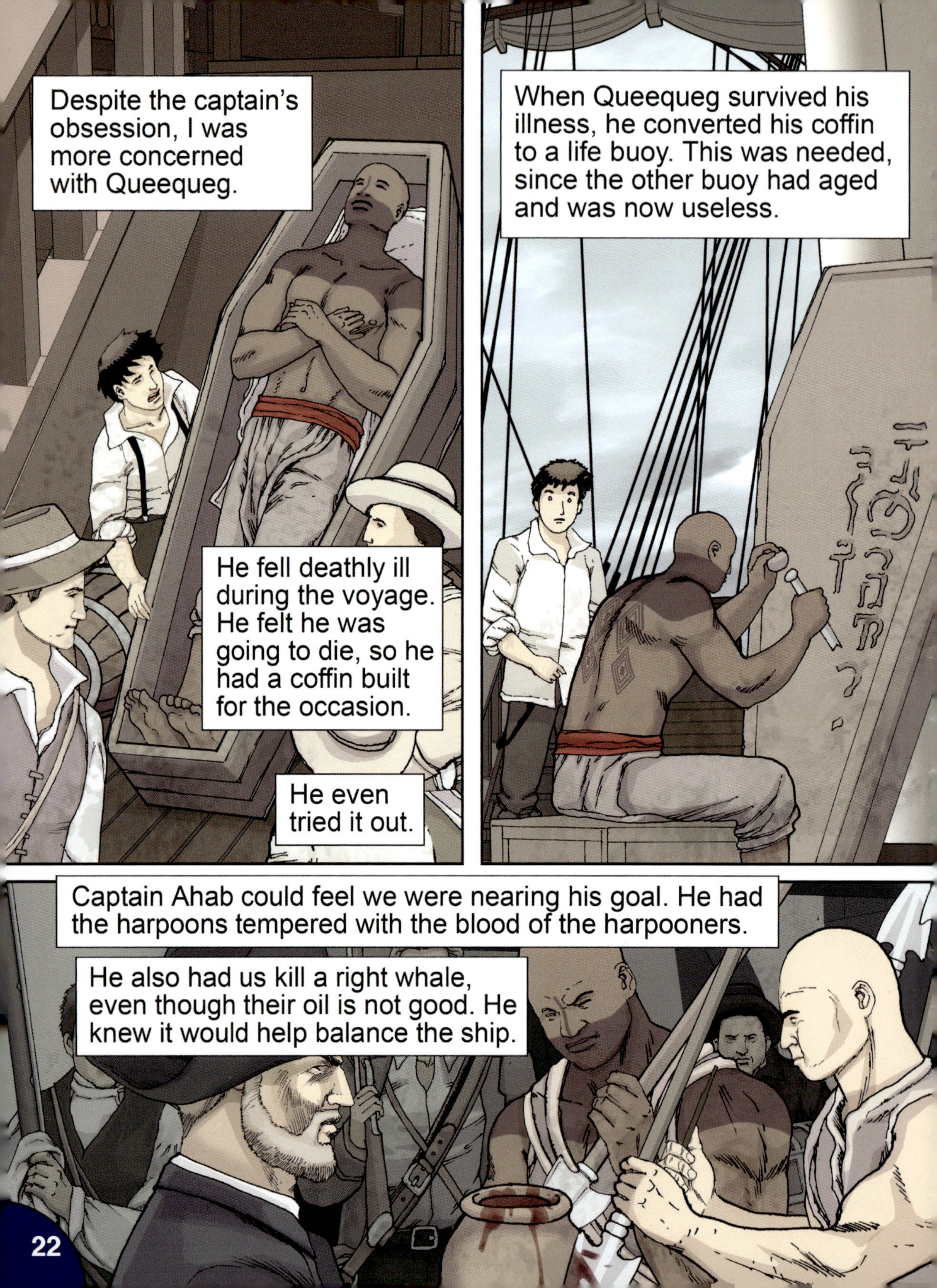
Despite the captain's obsession, I was more concerned with Queequeg.
He fell deathly ill during the voyage. He felt he was going to die, so he had a coffin built for the occasion.
He even tried it out.
When Queequeg survived his illness, he converted his coffin to a life buoy. This was needed, since the other buoy had aged and was now useless.
Captain Ahab could feel we were nearing his goal. He had the harpoons tempered with the blood of the harpooners.
He also had us kill a right whale, even though their oil is not good. He knew it would help balance the ship.

One day we came upon another ship, the *Rachel*.
WE FOUND YOUR WHITE WHALE AND WENT AFTER IT. IT DESTROYED ONE OF OUR BOATS.
IT WILL NOT GET AWAY FROM ME.
YOU HAVE TO HELP ME FIND MY SON. HE WAS ON THAT BOAT. I WILL EVEN PAY YOU!
NO! GET OFF MY SHIP, I AM LOSING PRECIOUS TIME.

Chapter 6 The Great White Whale
The race was now on to find the white whale.
THERE... THERE SHE BLOWS! MOBY DICK!
I HAVE SEEN IT FIRST, THE COIN IS MINE!
The chase was on.
The whale was fast, the fastest I had ever seen.
It disappeared beneath the waves. It had escaped.

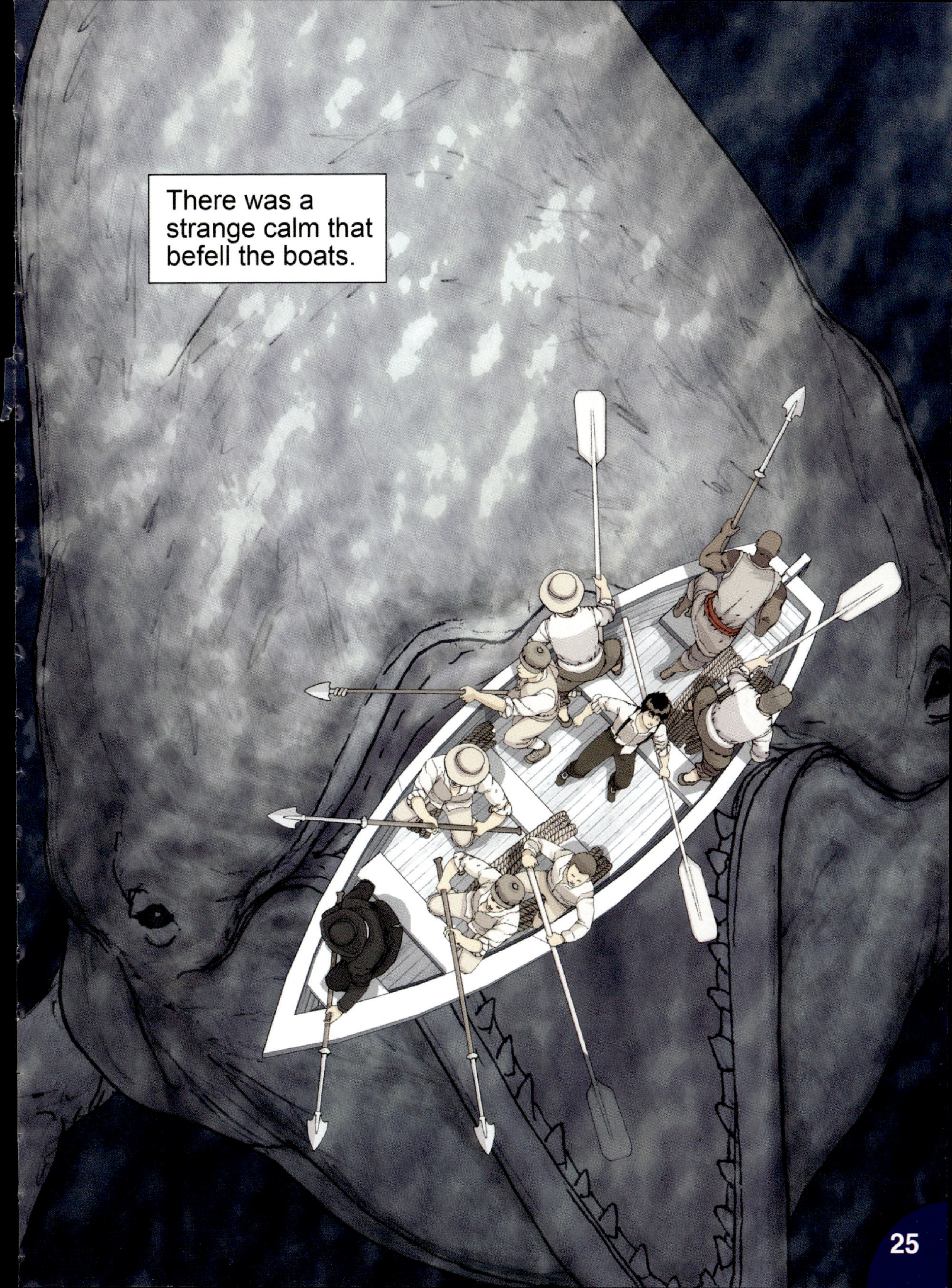
There was a strange calm that befell the boats.

Moby Dick then showed up.
The scars of previous battles
remained for all to see.

GO AFTER IT. DO NOT LET IT GET AWAY!
BUT SIR?
The captain was determined. He continued to press the attack.
The whale seemed to mock us.
It rammed the *Pequod* on the starboard bow!

TO THE LAST, I SHALL FIGHT THEE! IN HATE, I SHALL SPIT MY LAST BREATH AT THEE!

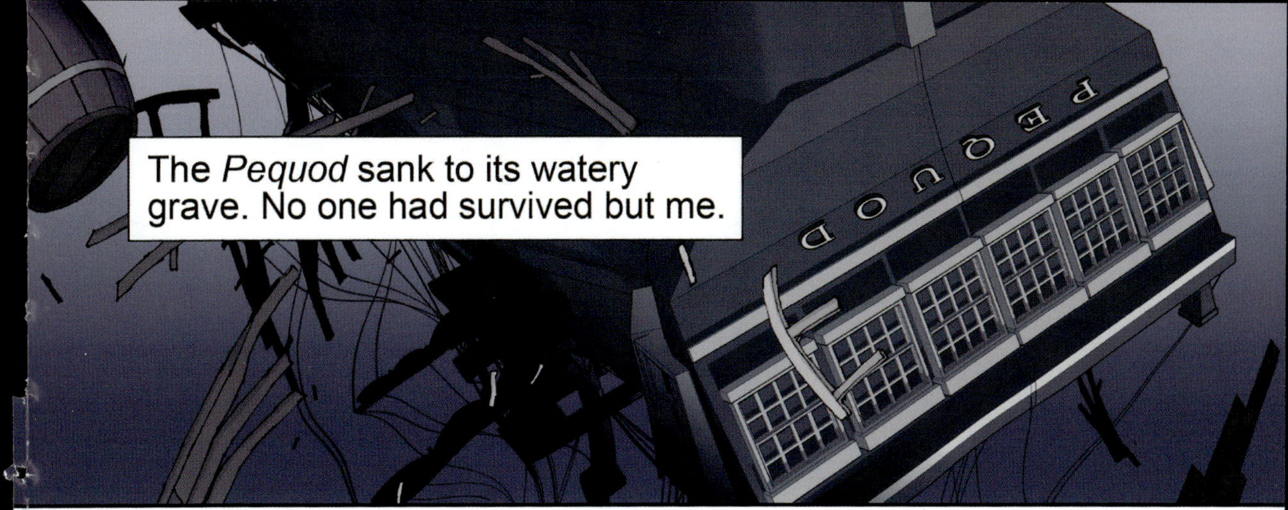
The *Pequod* sank to its watery grave. No one had survived but me.

The only reason I survived was because of the coffin Queequeg had built. Even in death, my best friend came to my aid.
For the next two days, my thoughts were of my friend and of Ahab's drive to death.

I was rescued by the *Rachel*, whose captain was still looking for his missing son. All they found was Ishmael, another orphan.

About the Author

Herman Melville was born on August 1, 1819, in New York City. He was the third of Allan and Maria Gansevoort Melvill's eight children. The family would later alter the spelling of their last name.

In 1826, Herman was ill with scarlet fever. The illness left him with weakened eyesight. Despite this, Herman attended Male High School. His father's business went bankrupt in 1830, and the family moved to Albany, New York.

Two years later, his father died. Melville tried to help support the family by taking various jobs. In 1839, he became a cabin boy on a ship sailing for Liverpool. This was the first of several sea voyages for Melville.

In 1844, Melville returned to his family with stories of his adventures. They encouraged him to write them down. His first book, *Typee*, was published in 1847. He quickly gained popularity, but many of his later works were not well received. Even his masterpiece, *Moby Dick*, was not successful during his lifetime.

Herman Melville died on September 28, 1891, with little recognition. He has since become one of the great American authors of the nineteenth century.

Additional Works

Other works by Herman Melville include

Typee (1846)
Omoo (1847)
Mardi (1849)
Redburn (1849)
White-Jacket (1850)
Israel Potter (1855)
Timoleon (1891)
Billy Budd (1924)

About the Adapter

Rod Espinosa is a graphic novel creator, writer, and illustrator. Espinosa was born in the Philippines in Manila. He graduated from the Don Bosco Technical College and Santo Tomas University.

Espinosa has worked in advertising, software entertainment, and film. Today, he lives in San Antonio, Texas, and produces stunning graphic novels including *Dinowars, Neotopia, Metadocs*, *Battle Girlz,* and many others. His graphic novel *Courageous Princess* was nominated for an Eisner Award.

Glossary

***blubber* -** a layer of fat in whales and other marine mammals. Blubber provides the whale with insulation, food storage, and padding.

***cannibal* -** one who eats the meat of its own kind.

***fluke* -** either of the fins that make up the tail of a cetacean, such as a whale or dolphin.

***harpoon* -** to strike or kill with a weapon resembling a spear that has a rope attached to it.

savage - a person belonging to a society or culture that is nonindustrial and often tribal.

***starboard* -** the right side of a ship when facing forward.

Web Sites

To learn more about Herman Melville, visit ABDO Publishing Company on the World Wide Web at www.abdopublishing.com. Web sites about Melville are featured on our Book Links page. These links are routinely monitored and updated to provide the most current information available.